To the spirit of sharing expressed
by so many individuals who gave their knowledge,
skill and time to help create this book;
and to that same spirit of sharing needed in all communities,
from the smallest family to the vast and magical
community of life on earth.

 Published by Advocacy Press
P.O. Box 236
Santa Barbara CA 93102 U.S.A.

Library of Congress Cataloging-in-Publication Data
Sheehan, Patty, 1945-
    Shadow and the ready time / text by Patty Sheehan : illustrations by Itoko Maeno
        p.   cm.
    Summary: A young female wolf must spend time learning many things before
she is ready to do all that grown-up wolves do. Includes discussion questions and
suggestions on ways to use the story.
    ISBN 0-911655-13-1 : $14.95
    1. Wolves – Juvenile fiction.   [1. Wolves – Fiction.]   I. Maeno.
Itoko. ill.   II. Title.
PZ10.3.S38524Sh   1994
[Fic]–dc20   94-10441
                                                                    CIP
                                                                    AC

Advocacy Press is a division of Girls Incorporated of Greater Santa Barbara,
an affiliate of Girls Incorporated.

Design & Typography, Cirrus Design

Printed in Hong Kong

SHADOW and the
Ready Time

Whitney —
A special story to share
with Hartley Elizabeth —
Love,
Mom and Dad

Christmas 1994

Written by **Patty Sheehan**

Illustrations by **Itoko Maeno**

Advocacy Press, Santa Barbara

SHADOW wanted to do everything the big wolves did.

One day, the big wolves howled the hunting song. AWOOO AWOOO AWOOO. Shadow howled as best she could. YIP YIP AWO WOOF YIP.

As the big wolves started toward the hill, she scampered at Papa Wolf's heels.

Suddenly, she felt Mama Wolf's jaws gently but firmly on the scruff of her neck. Shadow whimpered and lay down.

"Stay here with me," said Mama Wolf. "It will be the Ready Time for you to hunt when you're big and strong and can run fast."

After the big wolves had raced across the river into the forest, Shadow chased the other pups. She pounced on them and wrestled them to the ground. She played tug-a-bone with them and won.

"I *am* big and strong. I *can* run fast," thought Shadow, as she scrambled down the hill toward the river.

WOOF! WOOF! WOOF! Mama Wolf barked an alarm. "Run, Shadow! Eagle! Eagle!"

Shadow looked up just as the eagle swooped toward her. It knocked her over and Shadow tumbled into the river.

The waters churned over her and pulled her down. Shadow paddled and paddled. Her legs ached.

When she reached the surface, white foamy water banged her over rocks. Gasping for air, Shadow bobbed up and down as the wild river carried her farther and farther from her family.

After a long while the river calmed, and Shadow struggled onto the shore. Exhausted, she collapsed into a nest of leaves, and cried herself to sleep.

When Shadow woke up she found herself in a very strange place.

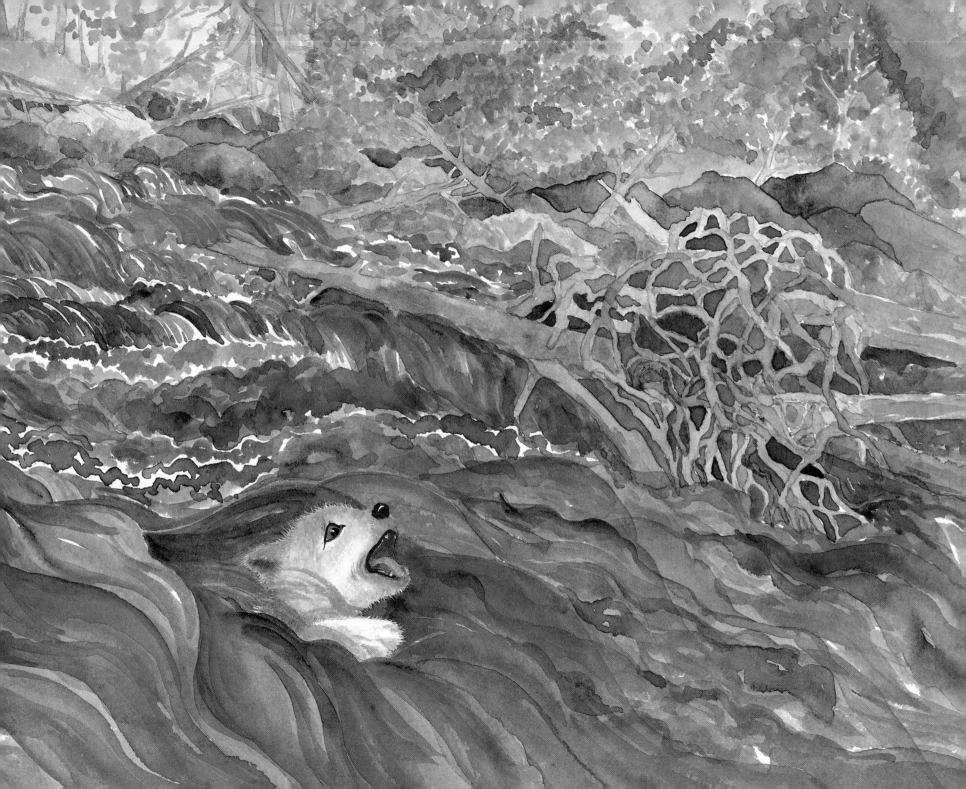

It had a fence around it.

"I want my family," Shadow whimpered to an old grey wolf who lay next to her.

"I know you do," the old wolf comforted. "But they are far away. The two-foot brought you here to me. I'll be your Nanna and take good care of you."

Nanna caressed Shadow's trembling body and fed her some meat. It soothed the hungry ache in Shadow's tummy.

The next day, Shadow felt better. She followed Nanna who limped up and down the hills and around the bushes.

"A moose antler tore my leg when I was hunting," Nanna said. Shadow shuddered.

Then Nanna grabbed a bone in her strong jaws. Shadow tugged and pulled. She felt the strength in her own jaws as she yanked the bone from Nanna's mouth.

Nanna pounced on a mouse that scurried across the ground and gulped it down. She swished her tail and Shadow pounced on it again and again, just as Nanna had pounced on the mouse. Soon Nanna growled. "Enough," and lay down.

Shadow grew bigger and stronger everyday, but she missed playing with the pups back home. "They play a much longer time than Nanna does before they rest," she thought.

The day Shadow pounced on a mouse and gulped it down, Nanna said, "It will soon be the Ready Time for you to hunt in the Freeplace." A chill of excitement ran up Shadow's spine. Then Nanna sighed. "With this bad leg, I'll never be able to run and hunt in the Freeplace. I can't go back with you," she said.

Shadow took Nanna's muzzle lightly in her mouth and kissed her.

As they curled close together, Shadow remembered the awful time when she was scared and hungry and lost. "I don't want to be alone. I'll have my own pups to play and snuggle with."

"First you must learn to take care of yourself," said Nanna. "Then find a pack of wolves to live with. You must learn to hunt with them and help them take care of their pups. Only then will it be the Ready Time for you to have your own."

Every evening, she told Shadow about the land and animals of the Freeplace.

Then one morning, Nanna said . . .

"Today the two-foot will take you to the Freeplace. Sometimes life will be hard. But you can learn everything you need to."

Shadow and Nanna howled together for a long time. AWOOO AWOOO. They nuzzled each other's noses to say good-bye.

After a long trip in the two-foot's truck, Shadow arrived in the Freeplace. She sniffed the fresh air and pricked her ears forward. Then Shadow bolted into the wind toward the woods.

A mouse scurried past her. Shadow pounced and gulped it down.

Until the next morning she hunted for mice. She caught a few and then, still hungry, Shadow curled up to rest with her nose under her tail.

"I wish I had pups to snuggle with," she thought, "but it's hard work finding food for just myself."

Shadow woke with a start. The scent of other wolves hung in the air.

AWOOO AWOOO AWOOO. Shadow howled. "I'm here. I want to live and hunt with you!"

Angry voices barked back.

"You're not strong enough or fast enough to hunt with us. This is our territory. Go away!"

Shadow's heart sank, and she ran deep into the woods. Suddenly she stopped short. Her heart pounded. There in front of her was a rushing river.

Trembling, Shadow remembered the terror of being swept away from her family so long ago. "Where can I go?"

Nanna's words echoed in Shadow's mind: "Sometimes life will be hard. But you can learn whatever you need to."

Cautiously Shadow stepped into the water. It pushed against her legs, but she was stronger than the river. She plunged in, swam to the other side, leapt onto a big rock, threw back her head and howled.

AWOOO AWOOO AWOOO. "I'll learn to be a great hunter."

The days grew longer and warmer. The snow melted away.

Sometimes Shadow felt lonely, but she loved to explore the woods and hills and valleys. She loved to chase rabbits and sleep under the bright stars in the big sky. She even loved to catch fish in the river.

Each day she ran farther and faster. Shadow's muscles grew stronger.

Then early one morning, a huge wolf ran out across the hilltop. He was dark as the night sky. Other wolves followed in his footprints.

A young wolf darted out of line after a rabbit. He ran as fast as the wind blew. "I'll catch the rabbit first," thought Shadow, and she raced neck and neck with the young wolf.

When the rabbit disappeared into the thicket, Shadow and the young wolf stopped to sniff each other, but the other wolves barked, "Wind, get back in line. Follow Night."

"His name is Wind," thought Shadow as the young wolf ran off. "And the leader of the pack is called Night."

Wind's glance said, "Follow us." Shadow's heart leapt at the sight of Wind's shining eyes, and she dashed after the pack.

But when they arrived atop a steep hill, Night barked at Shadow, "Don't come any closer. This is *our* home."

Then Night called out, "Moon, we've brought food." With tails wagging, a silver wolf and several pups ran to Night.

"The beautiful silver wolf is Moon," thought Shadow. Night fed the pups with food from his mouth while the other wolves dropped chunks of meat in front of Moon. After she ate, they sniffed her and licked her chin.

"Everyone loves Moon," thought Shadow. "She is a leader like Night. I wonder if I'll ever have pups and be a leader like Moon."

As Shadow sat deep in thought, she noticed something move on the top of the ledge. It was a pup!

An eagle circled above it!

WOOF! WOOF! WOOF! Shadow barked an alarm as she charged up the hill. "Run, little pup! Eagle! Eagle!"

Shadow sprang into the air and snapped at the eagle just as it swooped down at the pup. Screeching, the eagle flew away.

Moon herded the pup back to the den.

Then she barked at Shadow. "Come here." Shadow lowered her tail and head and trotted toward Moon.

"Thank you for saving my pup." Said Moon, "You may stay with us."

"Welcome," said the other wolves as they pranced around Shadow.

While Moon rested, the pups romped in the grass. They explored around the rocks. They jumped at butterflies. They dug holes in the dirt. Whenever a pup scampered off, Shadow herded it back.

Shadow flopped her tail for the pups to pounce on. She played tug-a-bone with them.

"You're good with the pups," said Moon. "I'll leave you in charge of them, so I can help the pack hunt food for us."

As the sun set, Moon and Night and Wind and the others sang the hunting song. AWOOO AWOOO AWOOO.

Wind sang the highest note. Then they bounded down the hill with Night and Moon in the lead.

Until late the next morning, Shadow played with the pups and kept them safe. Taking care of the pups was hard work, and when the pack returned, Shadow was very tired and very, very hungry.

Wind dropped some meat on the ground for Shadow. After she had eaten, Wind barked, "Come on Shadow, I'll race you to the meadow."

As she jumped toward him, Moon barked, "No! It's not the Ready Time for you and Wind to play together. Shadow, you will stay here and help me with the pups."

Shadow knew that Moon was not to be disobeyed, and so for many days to come Shadow cared for the pups.

26

One evening, Shadow tucked her tail between her legs and approached Moon. "I wish I had my own pups as you do," said Shadow.

"It is not the Ready Time for you to have pups," said Moon looking straight into Shadow's eyes. "A mother must always be sure her pups are cared for and have enough to eat. Other wolves help me because I'm a strong hunter, and I have taught them to hunt."

Then Moon added, "Tonight Wind will watch the pups, and we'll teach you to hunt with us." Shadow wagged her tail and ran to the howling circle.

AWOOO AWOOO AWOOO. She sang with the others and bounded down the hill after them. On the hilltop, Wind was already busy chasing the pups through the tall grasses.

29

Shadow dashed after the pack. She had never run so far or so fast. The smell of prey filled her nostrils. The wolves forged into a clearing and surrounded an enormous old moose.

Shadow charged toward the moose, but it lowered its head and Shadow leapt back frightened by the big antlers.

Shadow watched as the pack brought the moose to the ground. Her mouth watered, but Night snarled, "You must wait until we've eaten."

"I have a lot to learn," thought Shadow. "I'll watch Moon and Night and practice everything they do." For many evenings to come Shadow ran with the pack, growing braver and more skilled with each hunt.

Then one day, snow fell. "The coldtime is here," said Moon. "We must leave the ledge in search of food. The pups are big and strong now. They can travel with us."

Everyone howled the hunting song. Shadow harmonized with Wind as he sang the highest note.

Then, the pack began a life of following the elk and moose and deer down the valley, and sleeping wherever they found shelter from the blasting snow.

When the pack hunted, Shadow and Wind ran with the pups at the end of the line, herding them back whenever they straggled or strayed.

Wind would say, "Watch Moon and Night. And practice what they do."

When there were no big animals to hunt, Shadow taught the pups to catch mice and chase down rabbits.

Through that long and hard coldtime Shadow's muscles grew solid. She became one of the pack's best hunters, and they now allowed her to eat with them.

When another warmtime and another coldtime had passed, Shadow had learned to hunt as well as Moon and Night.

Then, when the sun warmed the earth again, all the wolves agreed that Shadow and Wind had become the strongest hunters of all. With lowered ears and tails they licked Shadow's and Wind's chins to tell them, "You are now our leaders."

From that day on, Shadow and Wind played together after the hunts. They snuggled and groomed each other more and more each day. And they mated.

One morning, Shadow dug out a cozy den.

Wind wagged his tail and took her muzzle gently in his mouth. Shadow wagged her tail and entered the den.

There inside she lay down to rest.

Day after day, Wind dropped meat inside the den for Shadow. Day after day, he howled with the other wolves right by the entrance to the den.

At last, Shadow's time came. Wind poked his head inside the den and backed out silently. Moments later, Shadow heard him howl from the top of the ledge.

AWOOO AWOOO AWOOO. "They're here," he sang.

AWOOO AWOOO. They're all fine."

AWOOO AWOOO AWOOO. The other wolves harmonized in their song of joy. Wind sang the highest note.

Nanna's words echoed in Shadow's mind: "You must learn to hunt with them and help them take care of their pups. Only then . . . ."

Shadow licked each of her very own tiny pups clean. She curled around them and gave them milk. "You came at the perfect time," Shadow whispered.

"The Ready Time!"

Dear Parents and Educators:

Shadow And The Ready Time accurately reflects much about how wolves live in harmony with each other and their environment. They live and hunt for food in packs. The adults teach the young all the skills necessary for adulthood. Only the strongest hunters and best leaders become parents, and when food is in short supply, they will have small or no litters. Both parents, along with help from pack members, raise the young.

In a world of rapidly increasing population and depleting resources, perhaps wolf culture can indicate how we and future generations can enjoy life's privileges and freedoms.

To help children understand the story, here are some questions to think and talk about together:

- Why did Mama Wolf tell Shadow it wasn't the Ready Time for her to hunt?
- When Nanna said she could not go with Shadow to the Freeplace, why did Shadow say she wanted to have pups?
- Why didn't the first wolves Shadow heard in the Freeplace want Shadow to be in their pack?
- Why was Shadow invited by Moon to stay with her pack?
- What were some of the things Shadow learned to do after she joined the pack?
- What might have happened to Shadow if she had had pups before she belonged to a pack?
- Are there some things you would like to do that you aren't ready yet to do? What are they?
- Do you think you will want to have children someday?
- How can you become ready for these experiences? What help will you need from others?

Young people today experience a lot of peer pressure to grow up quickly. Many become parents before they are prepared to adequately feed, house or provide guidance to their children.

Premature sexual behavior and becoming a teen parent are often misguided attempts to meet needs for: self-esteem; sense of importance; touch and affection; nurturing others; a sense of belonging; making a contribution; finding meaning and purpose. To help young people assume responsibility for meeting their needs in healthy ways, and for the fulfillment of their dreams:

- Exhibit pride in their accomplishments, remembering that even seemingly insignificant play activities contribute to greater and greater competencies later on. If children feel acknowledged for who they are and what they can do as children, they are less driven to prove self-worth by demonstrating inappropriate adult behaviors.
- Encourage them to develop their abilities and interests.
- Find ways for them to contribute to environmental, social and other causes.
- Teach them to care for younger children, pets, and plants.
- Encourage new games, contact sports, dance and other activities where they can touch or show affection. And remember we all need hugs!
- Cooperate with other parents to assure a variety of supervised group activities.
- Give them the amount and type of choices they can responsibly handle.
- Let them enjoy the results of positive behavior and hold them responsible for mistakes they make.
- Teach boys as well as girls that they are responsible for any lives they help create.
- Let children know you want to talk with them about sexuality and any other concerns they may have about growing up. Answer their questions honestly, in a relaxed manner without elaborating on information not requested.
- When you don't know the answers to their questions, help them find answers.
- Enroll them in school and community programs that teach about sexuality, pregnancy and parenting as well as educational and career opportunities. Be sure to "check out" the content of these programs first.
- To involve teenagers in the message of the *Ready Time,* ask them to share the story with younger children. Perhaps together they could read and discuss it.

About the Author

Patty Sheehan is a psychotherapist, speaker, and teacher who helps adults and children to develop personally and in their relationships. Patty has a master's degree in education and is the author of three earlier books for children *Kylie's Song, Kylie's Concert* and *Gwendolyn's Gifts*, all of which help children nurture their individual gifts. Now in *Shadow and the Ready Time,* she encourages children to take time for their own development before assuming such adult responsibilities as parenting. Patty lives in Albuquerque, New Mexico, near the Sandia Mountains, where she enjoys friends, activities, and participation in environmental causes. Her concern for people and all of nature is reflected in *Shadow and the Ready Time.*

About the Illustrator

Itoko Maeno is one of the nation's leading children's book illustrators, and has over a dozen to her credit. She has illustrated the entire award winning Advocacy Press Self-Esteem Series which includes *Minou, Kylie's Song, My Way Sally, Tonia the Tree* and *Time for Horatio.* She also illustrated the charming *Mother Nature Nursery Rhymes* and *Nature's Wonderful World in Rhyme.* Itoko also provided many of the illustrations for the beautiful, best-selling series of Choices Journal/Workbooks for Self-awareness and Personal Planning for teens and young adults. Born in Tokyo, Japan, Itoko received her B.A. in Graphic Design from Tama University.

Books Published By Advocacy Press

Illustrated Children's Books

Berta Benz and the Motorwagen

Father Gander Nursery Rhymes

Kylie's Song

Mimi Makes a Splash

Mimi Takes Charge

Minou

Mother Nature Nursery Rhymes

My Way Sally

Nature's Wonderful World in Rhyme

Shadow and the Ready Time

Tonia the Tree

Choices Series

Making Choices for Teen Boys and Girls

Choices: A Teen Woman's Journal for Self-awareness and Personal Planning

Challenges: A Young Man's Journal for Self-awareness and Personal Planning

More Choices: A Strategic Planning Guide for Mixing Career and Family

Changes: A Woman's Journal for Self-awareness and Personal Planning

Career Series

FOODWORK Jobs in the Food Industry and How to Get Them

You can find these books at better bookstores. Or you may send for a free catalog from Advocacy Press, P.O. Box 236, Dept. S, Santa Barbara, CA 93102.

the Big Sky Country

Huckleberry

BRITISH COLUMBIA   ALBERTA   CANADA

U.S.A.

WASHINGTON   NORTH DAKOTA

IDAHO   MONTANA

Bitterroot

OREGON   SOUTH DAKOTA
Common Harebell

Indian Paintbrush   WYOMING

Lupine   Bunchberry
Dogwood

Nuttall Violet